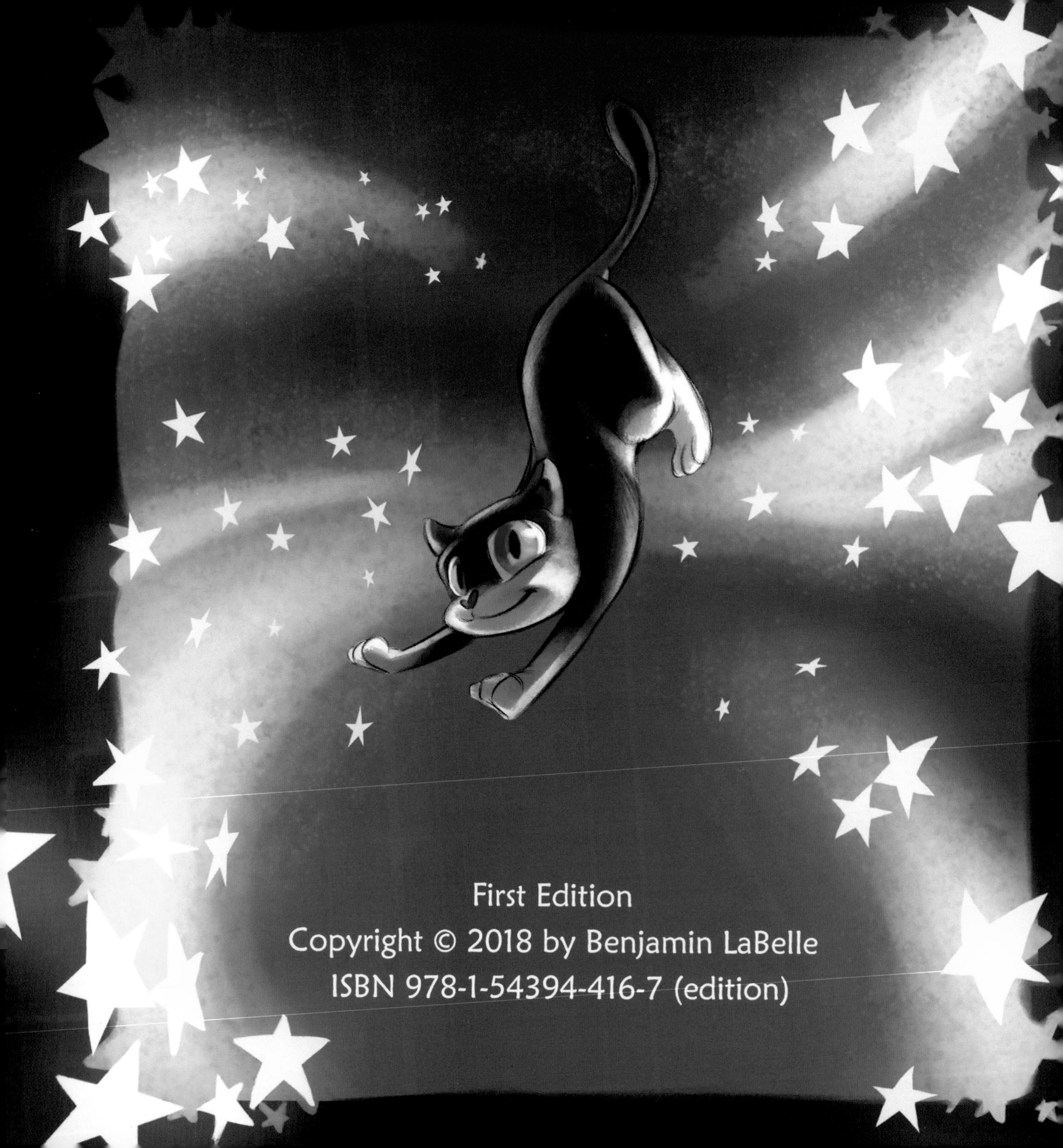

First Edition

ISBN 978-1-54394-416-7 (edition)

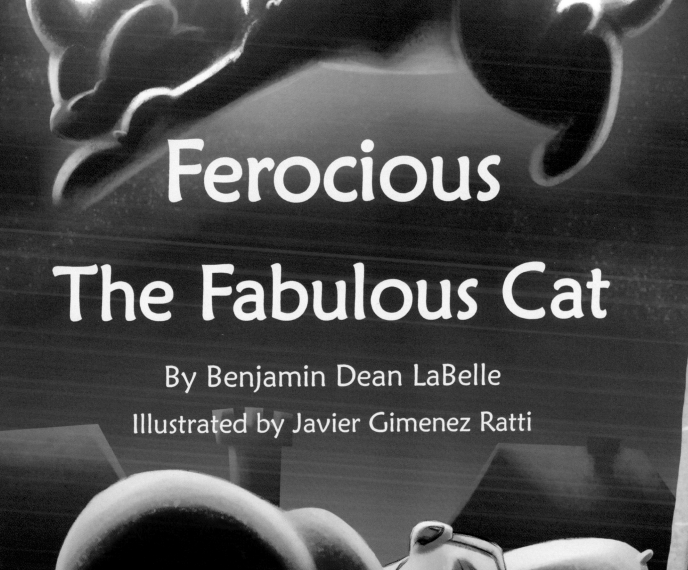

Ferocious

The Fabulous Cat

By Benjamin Dean LaBelle

Illustrated by Javier Gimenez Ratti

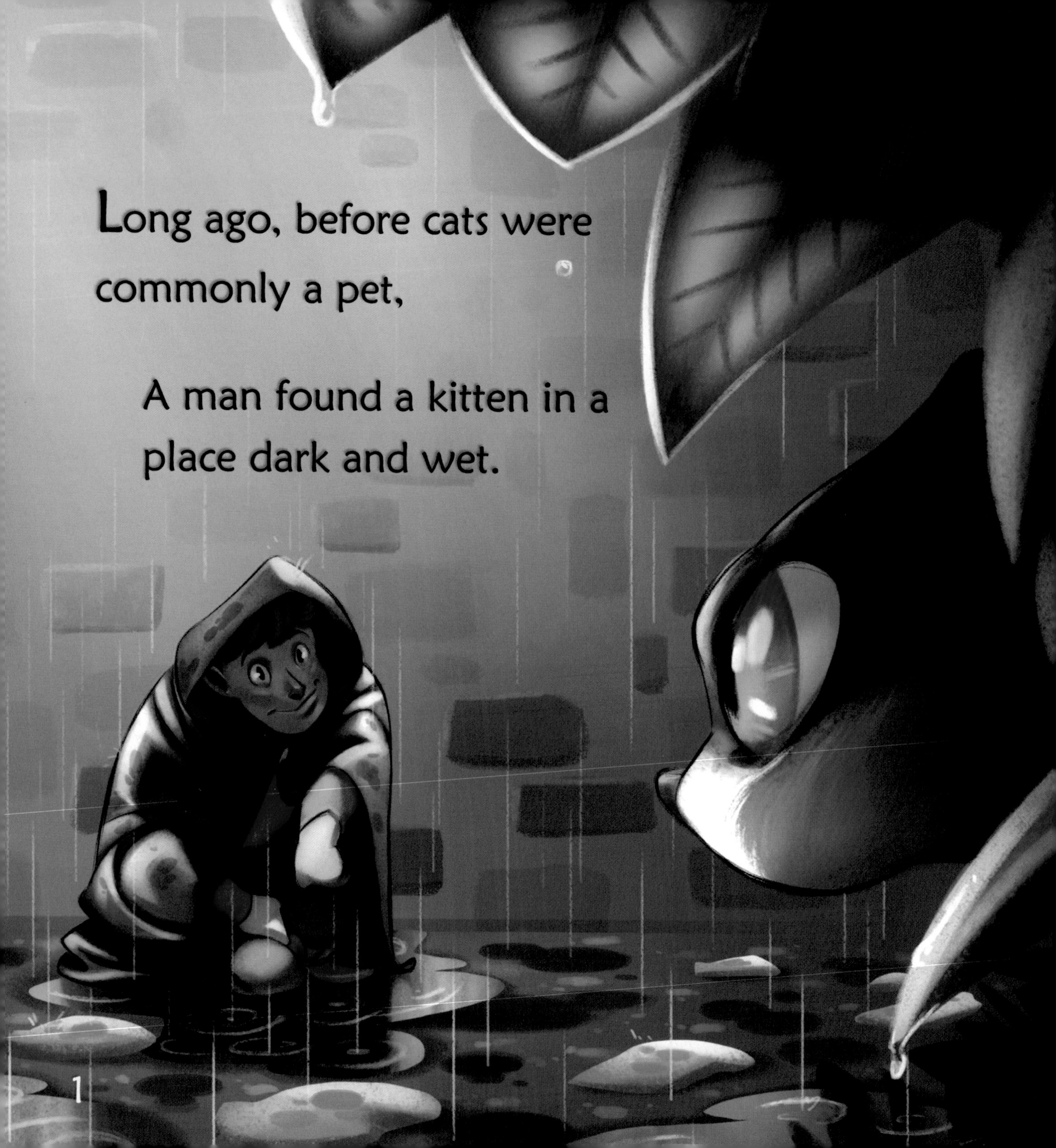

Long ago, before cats were commonly a pet,

A man found a kitten in a place dark and wet.

He quickly scooped her up
and their eyes met.

At that moment, the two
became an inseparable duet.

He named her Ferocious,
as she was crazy
and fun.

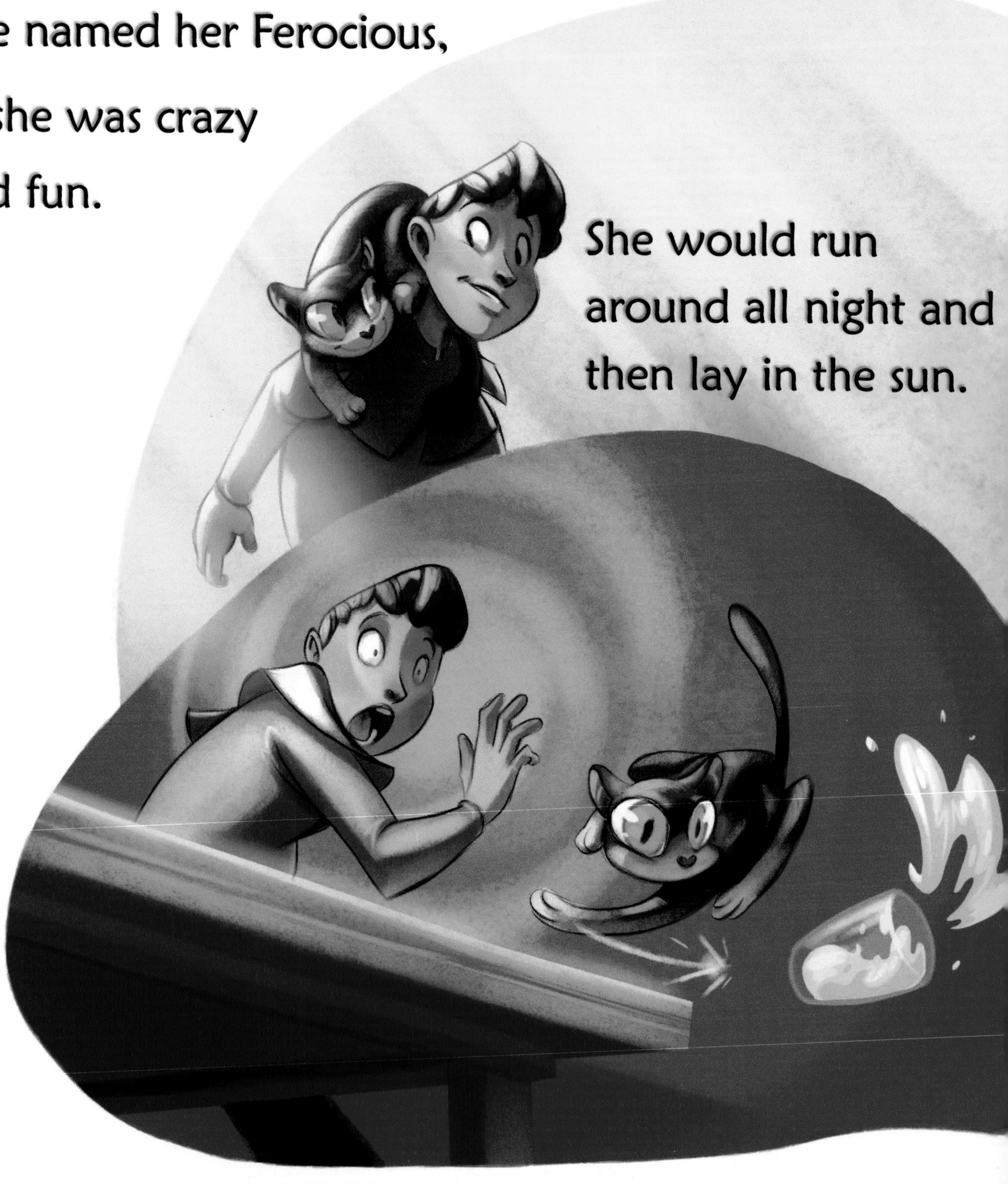

She would run
around all night and
then lay in the sun.

She was elegant, intelligent and oh so curious.

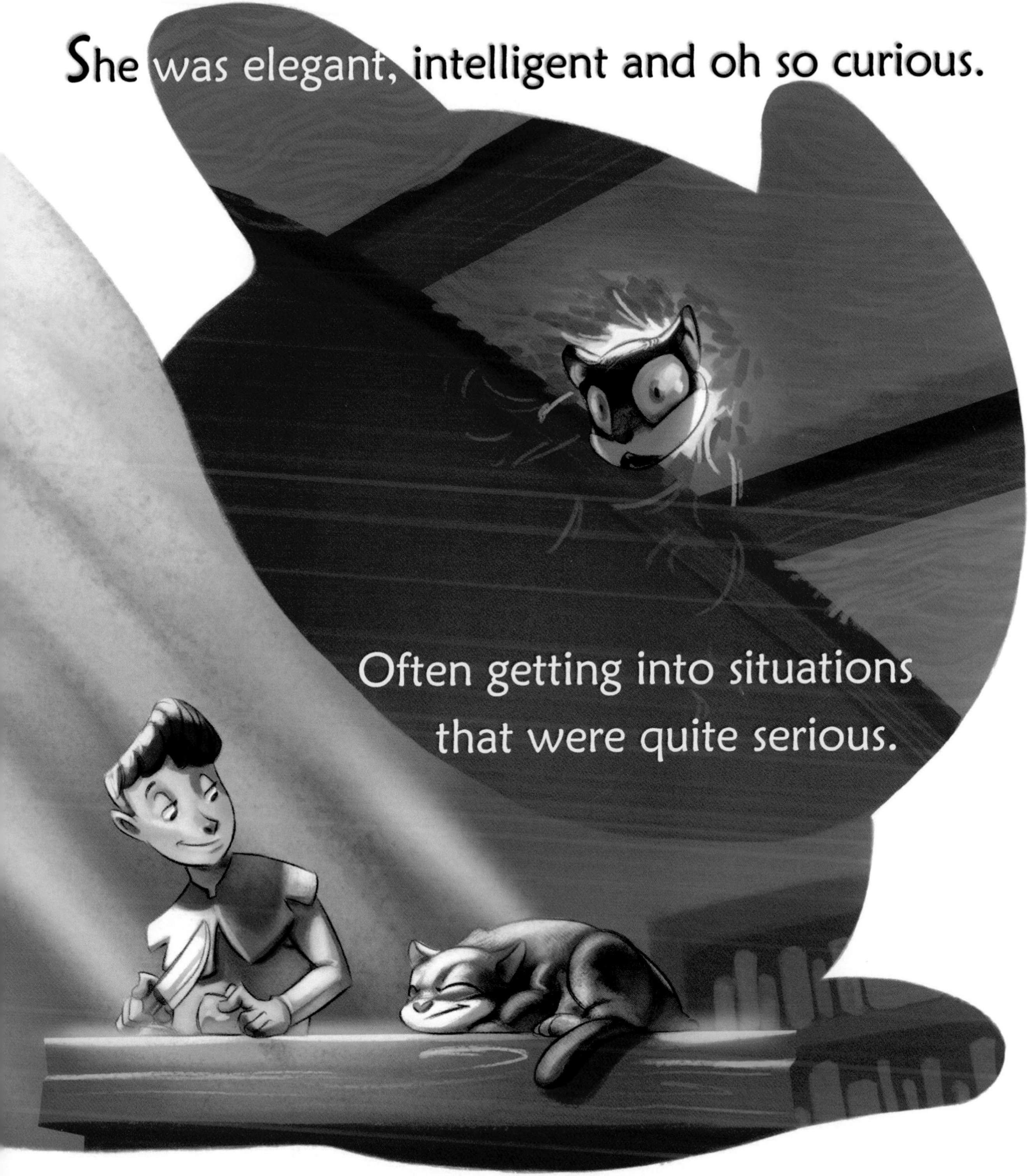

Often getting into situations
that were quite serious.

She had weird habits, like puking hairballs the size of pies,

Playing and talking with the man in loud obnoxious cries.

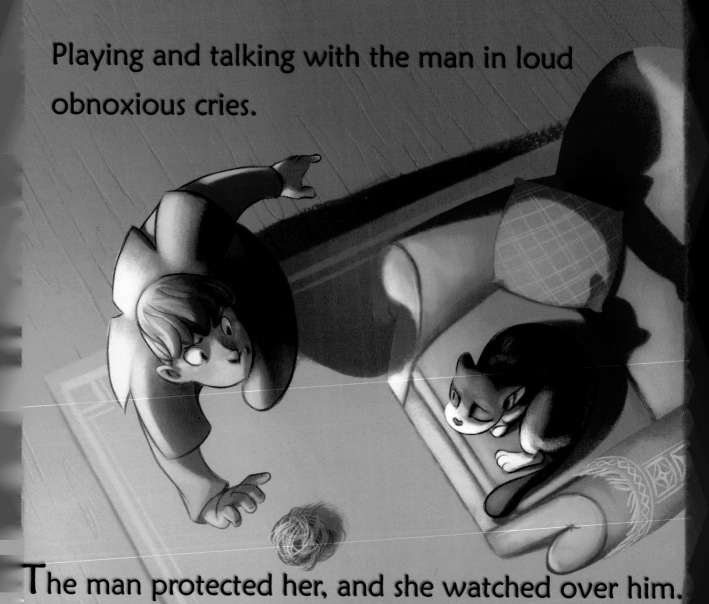

The man protected her, and she watched over him.

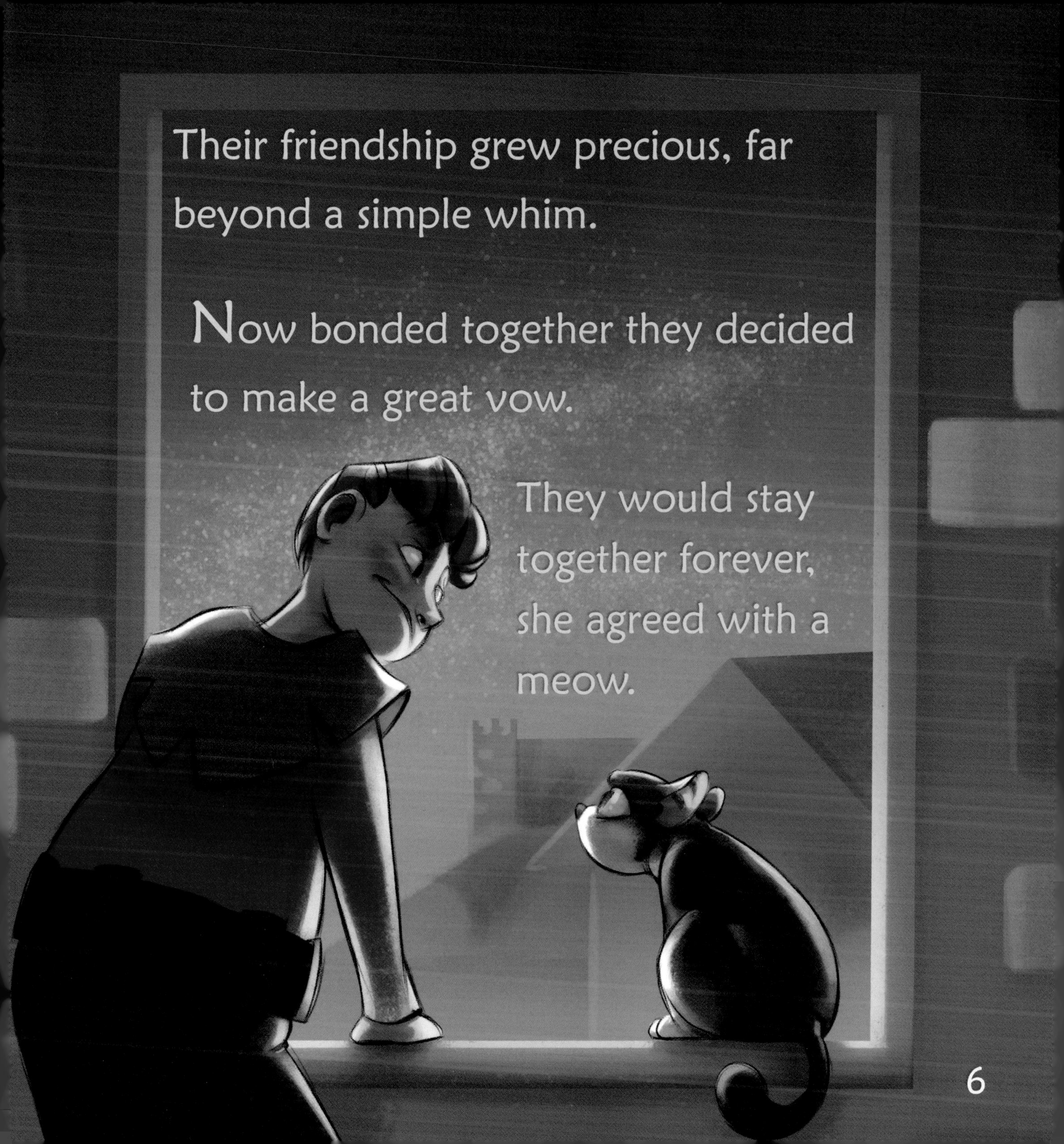

Their friendship grew precious, far beyond a simple whim.

Now bonded together they decided to make a great vow.

They would stay together forever, she agreed with a meow.

Now this was a time long ago, when darkness would haunt people where they did live.

It would make good people do the opposite of love and give.

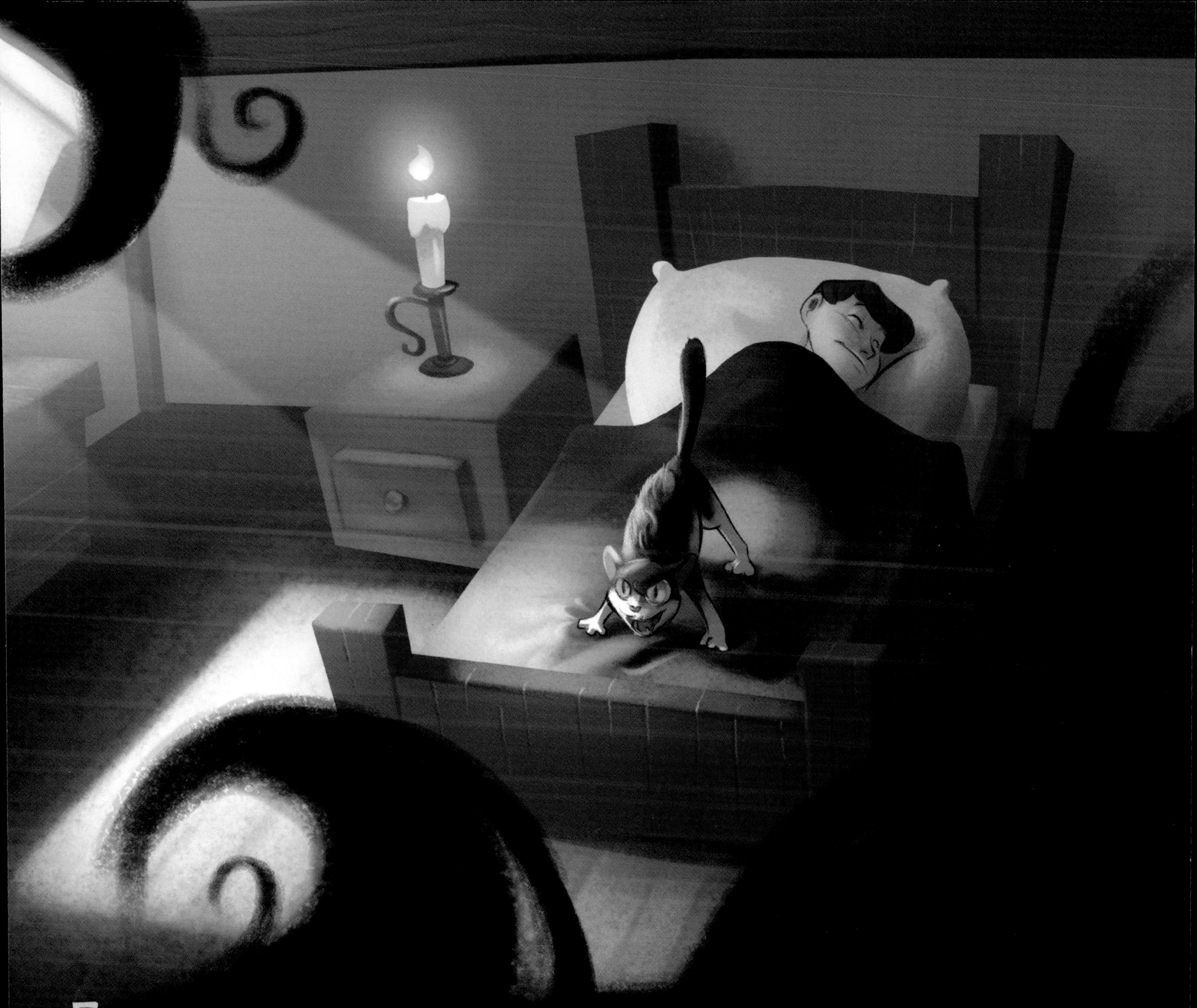

Ferocious one night, was snuggling her man close.

When she saw this darkness on a fast approach.

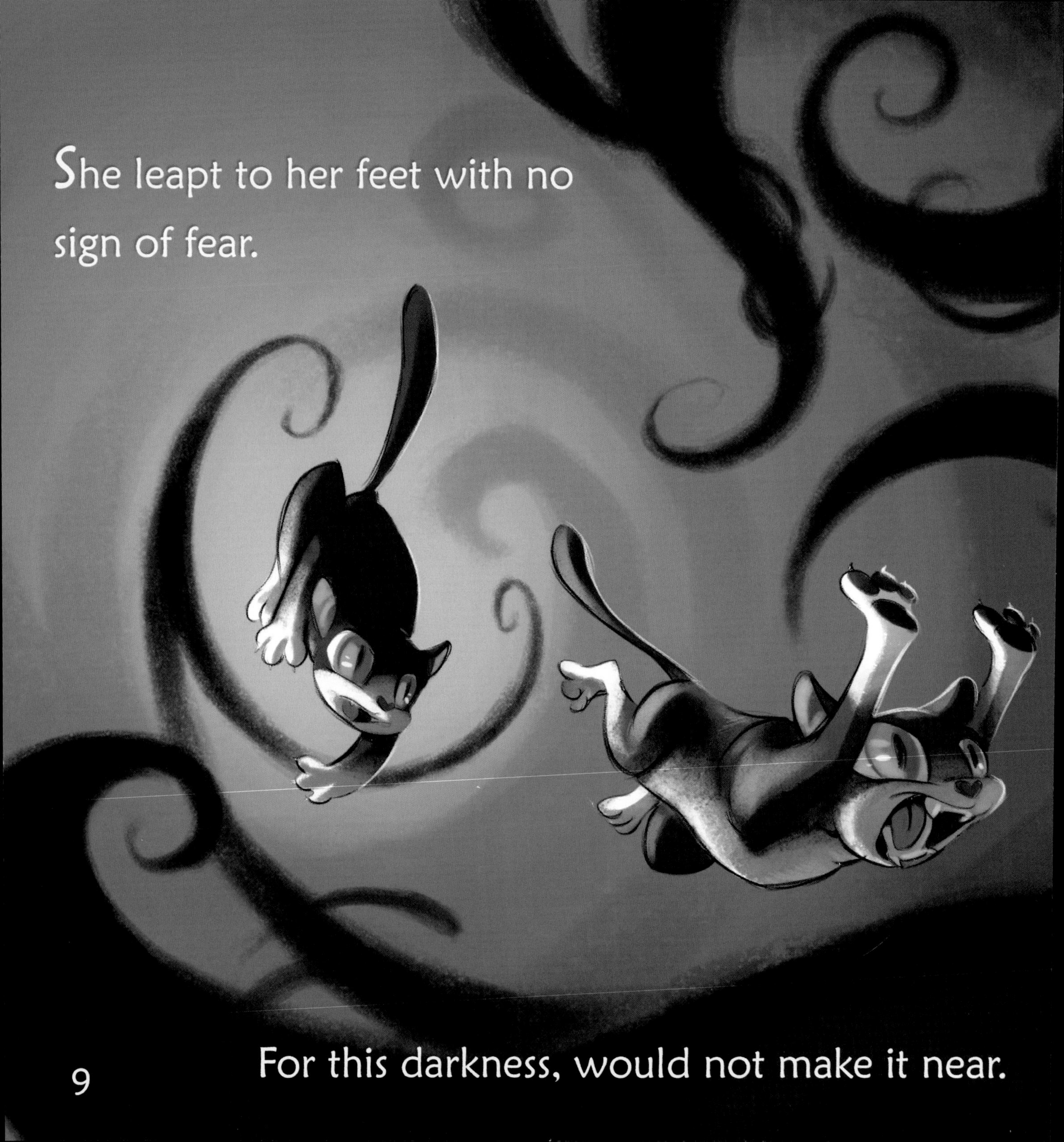

She leapt to her feet with no sign of fear.

For this darkness, would not make it near.

Her eyes blazed green and she gave a great growling shout.

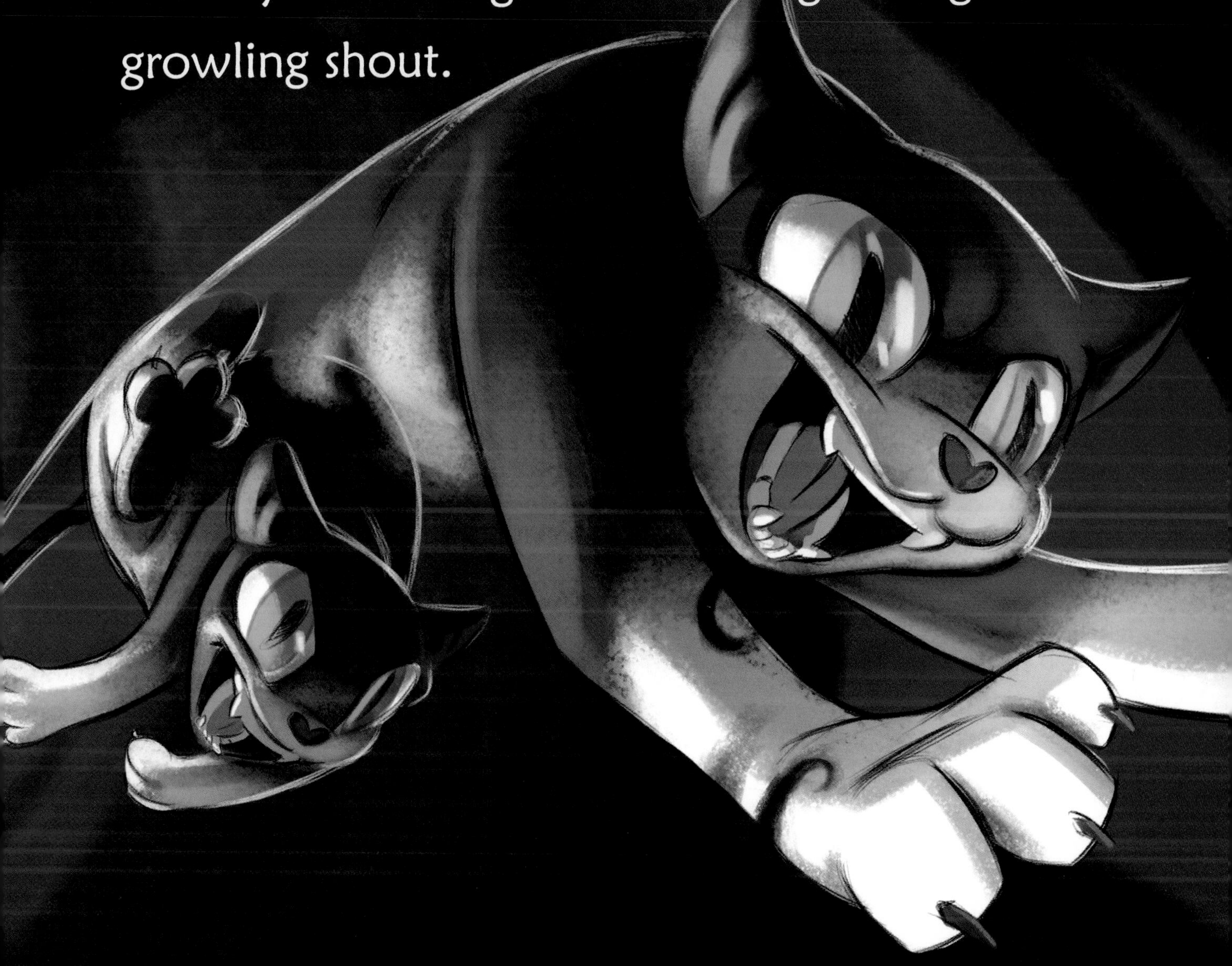

She quickly attacked with her paws, swatting that darkness right out.

For no darkness, would touch her precious friend.

Every night she would stay close, cuddled tight to defend.

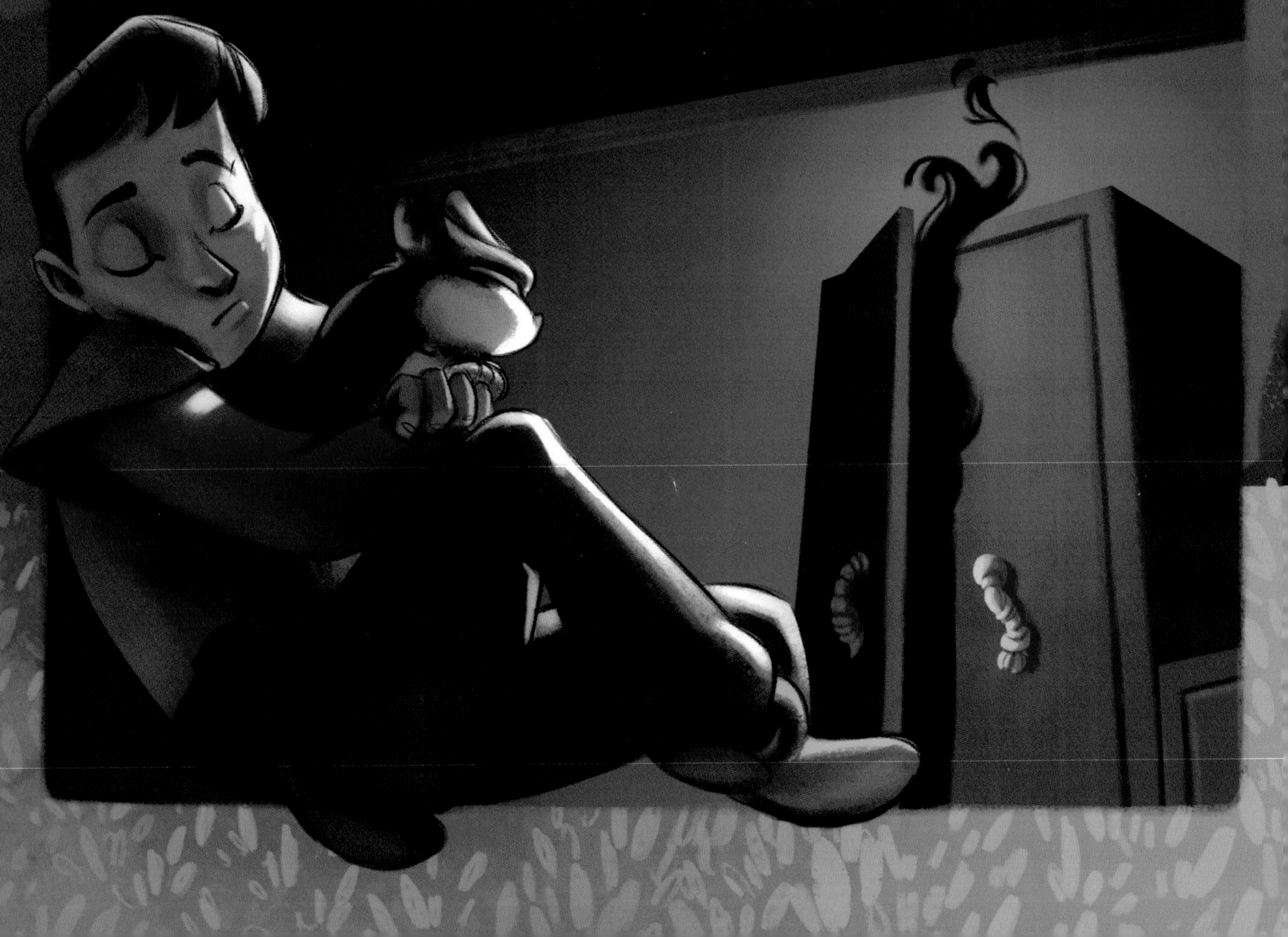

As time went on, the man met a woman with a kind and gentle touch.

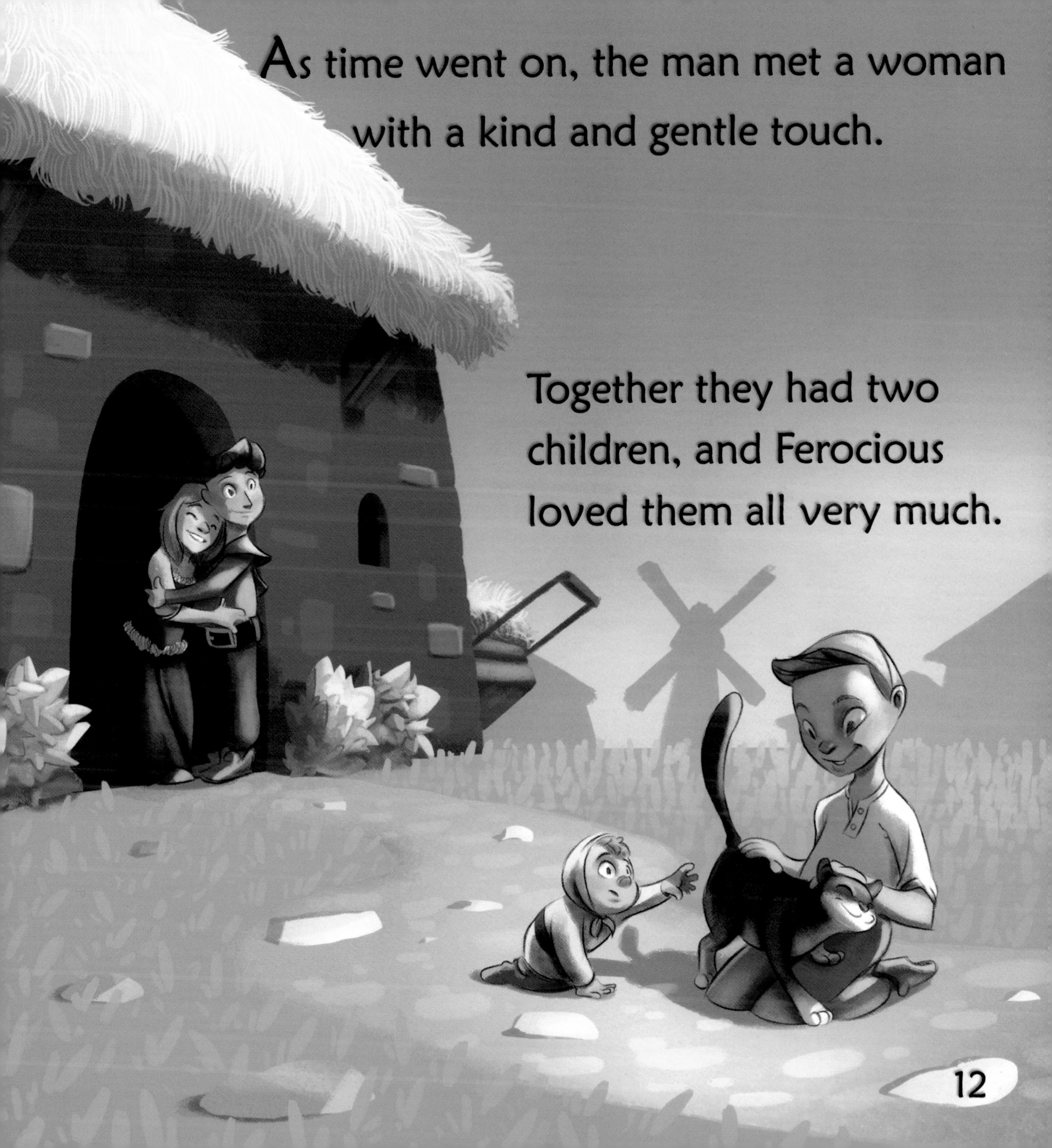

Together they had two children, and Ferocious loved them all very much.

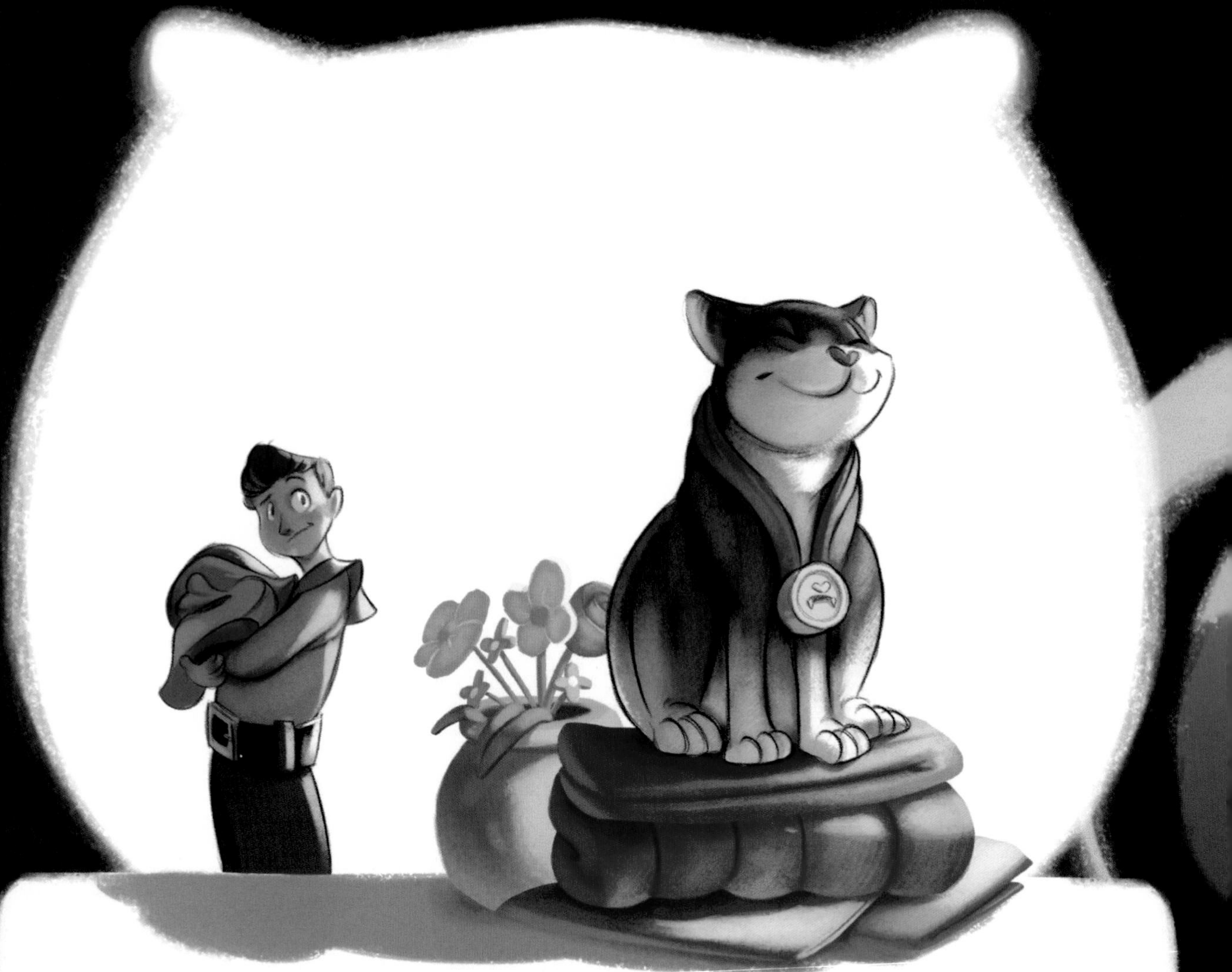

She grew stronger to protect her family, honoring that great vow.

With a regal stature, blazing eyes, and great and mighty meow.

Every night she continued snuggling her loves tight.

Making sure all was well and all was right.

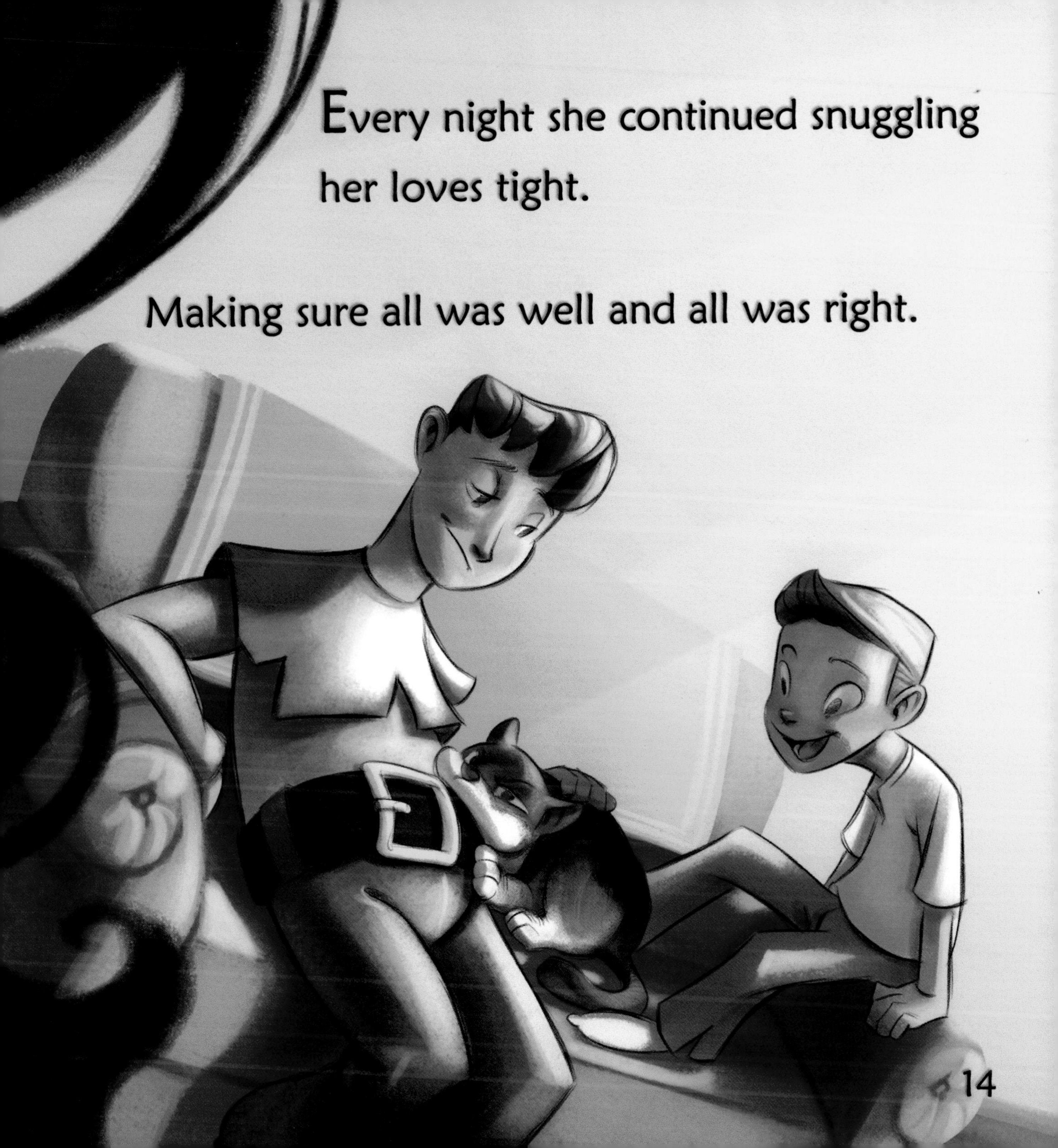

But as things do, Ferocious started to age.

Little by little her body became a cage.

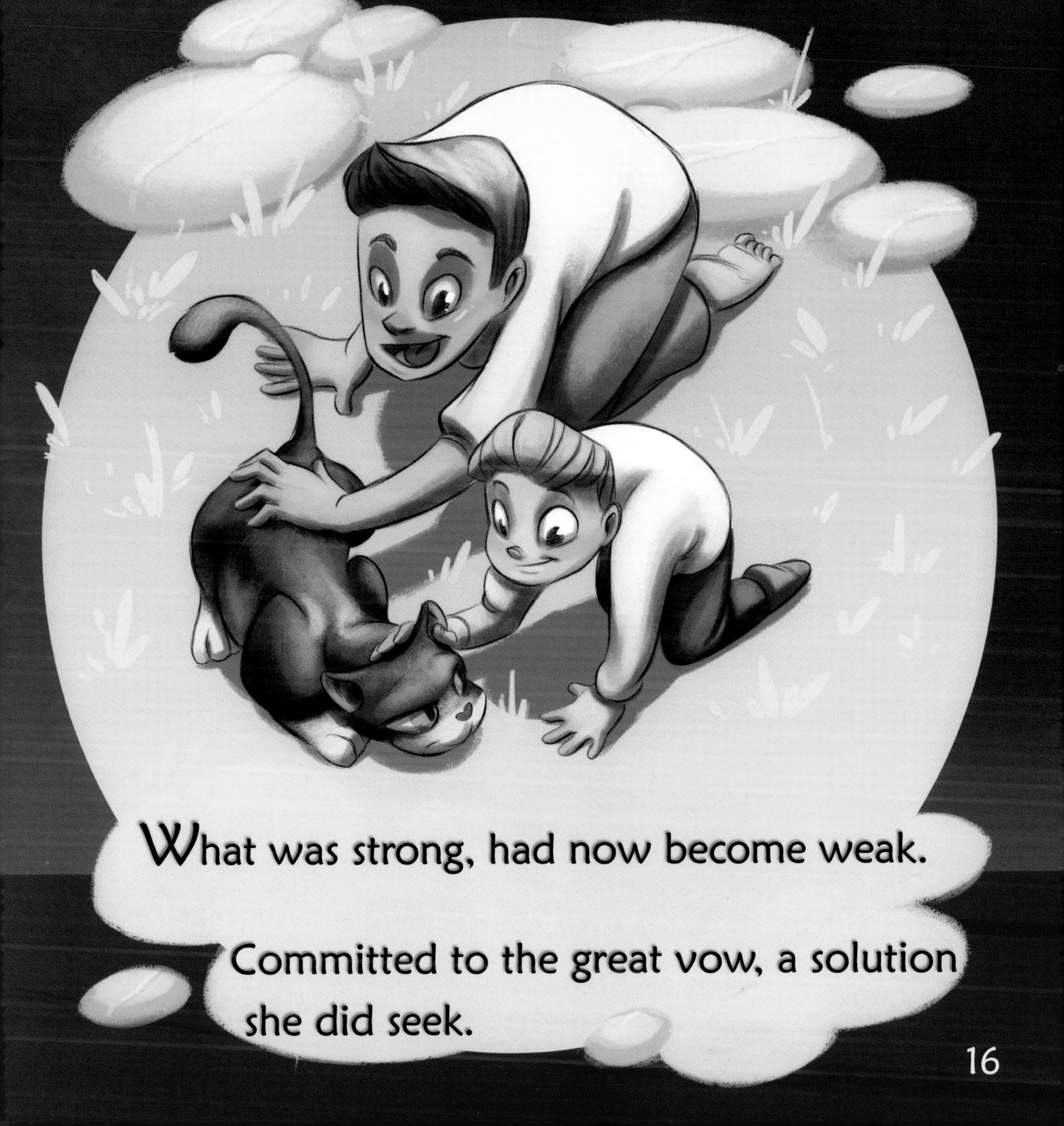

What was strong, had now become weak.

Committed to the great vow, a solution she did seek.

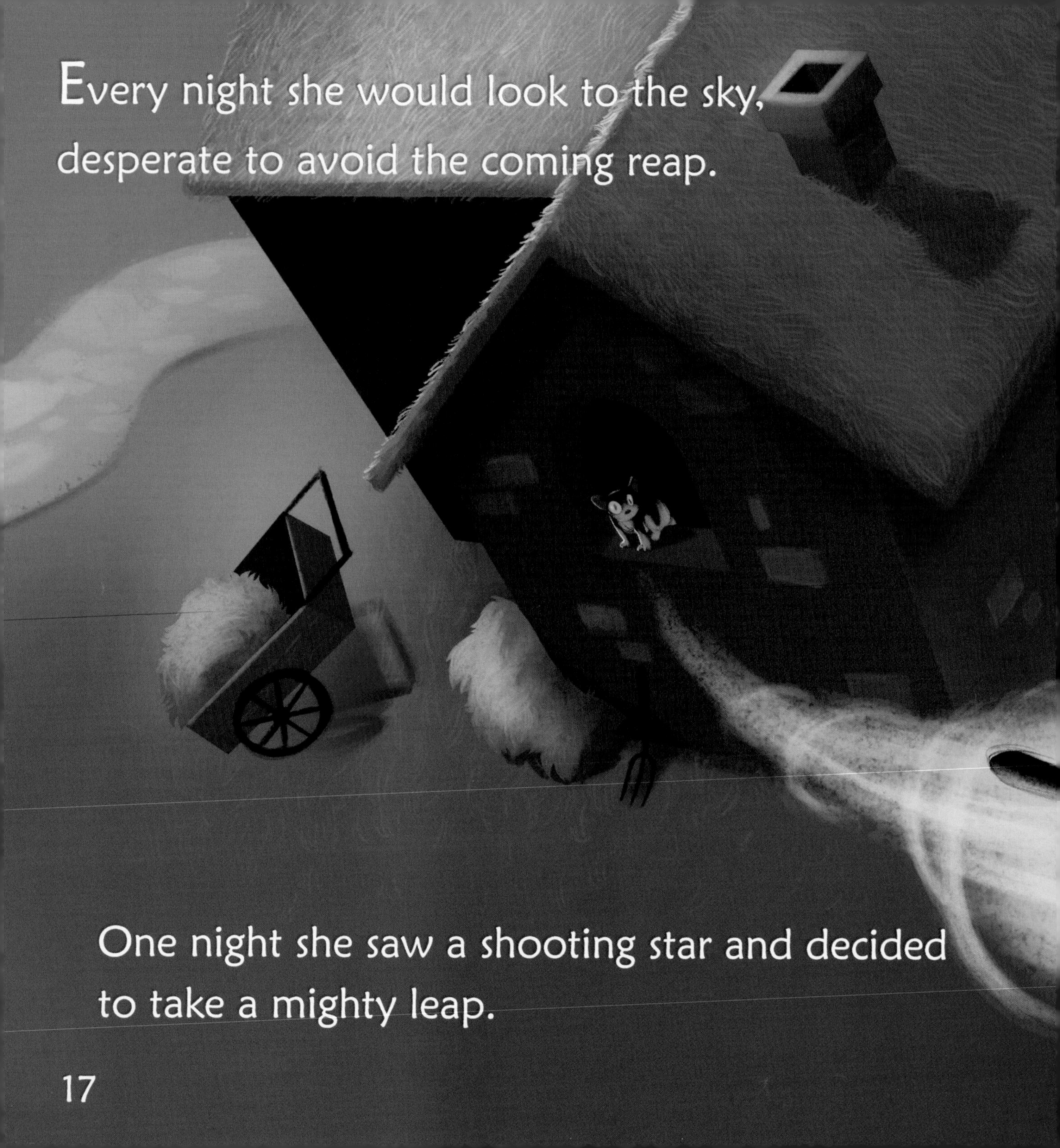

Every night she would look to the sky, desperate to avoid the coming reap.

One night she saw a shooting star and decided to take a mighty leap.

To the stars, she shot with her eyes blazing green.

She journeyed higher than any had ever seen.

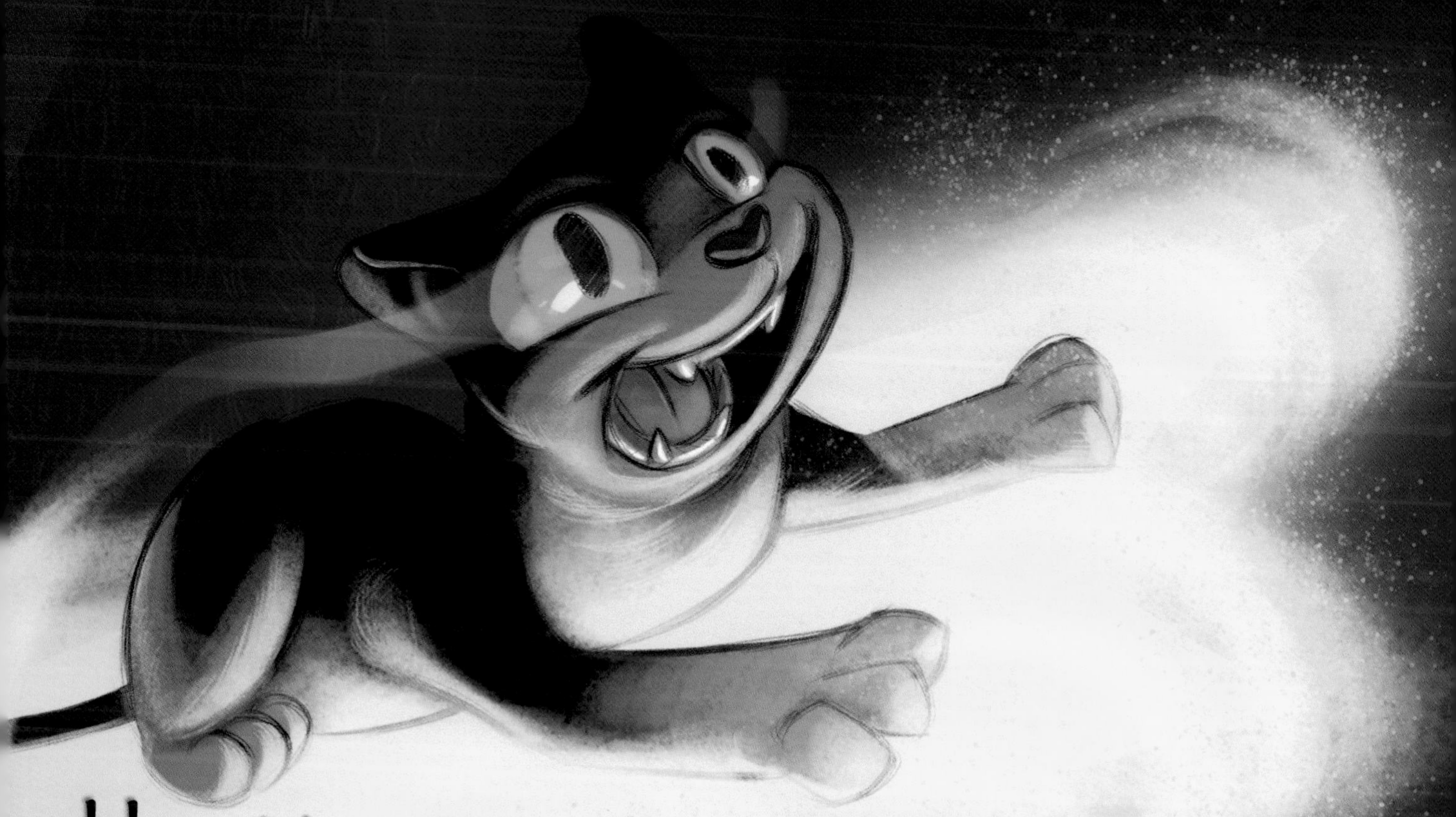

Her mighty meow echoed through the heavens above.

Delivered as a warning to the darkness, she will be protecting all with love.

There she became one with the stars, watching over us all every single night.

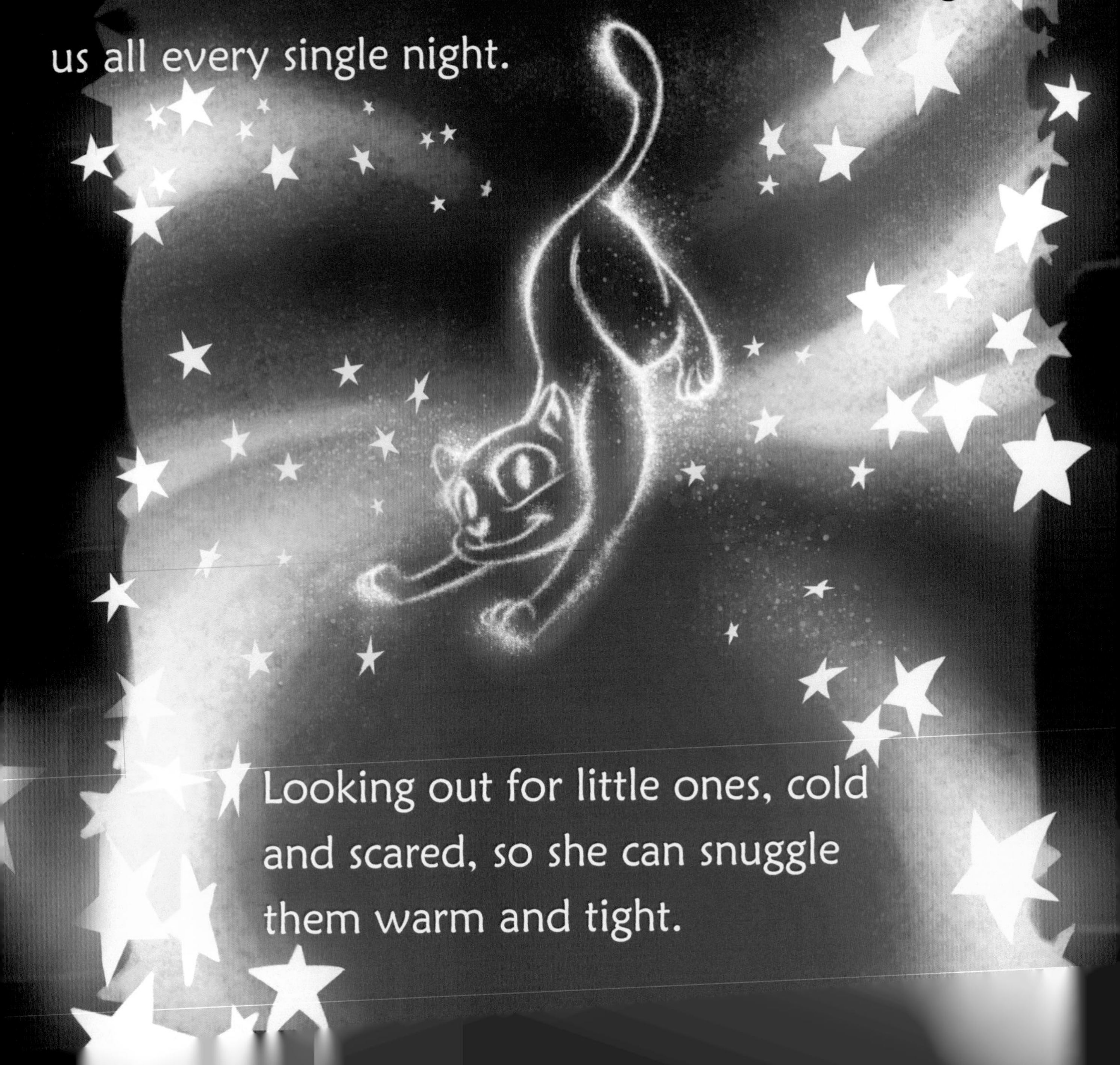

Looking out for little ones, cold and scared, so she can snuggle them warm and tight.

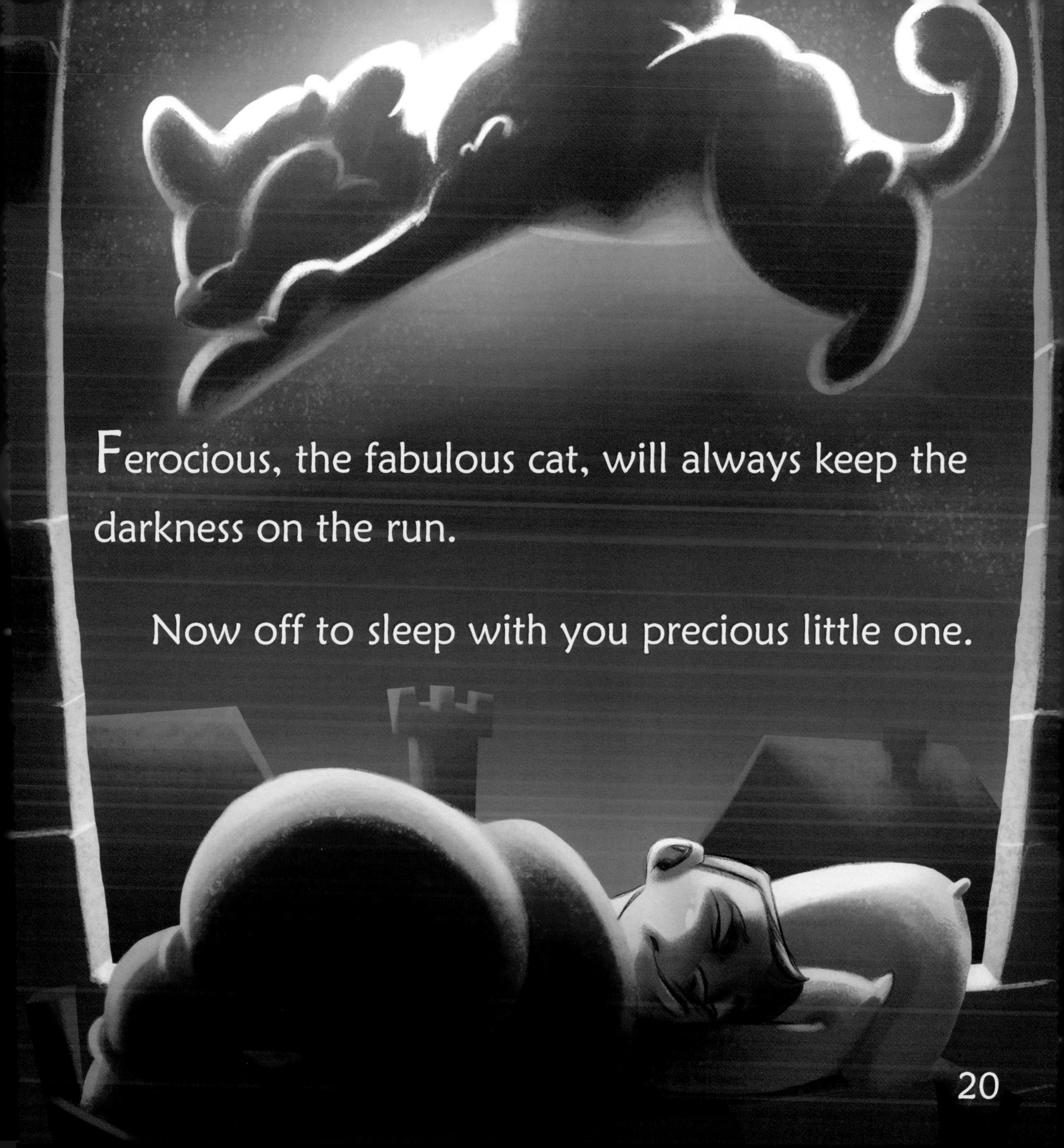

Ferocious, the fabulous cat, will always keep the darkness on the run.

Now off to sleep with you precious little one.

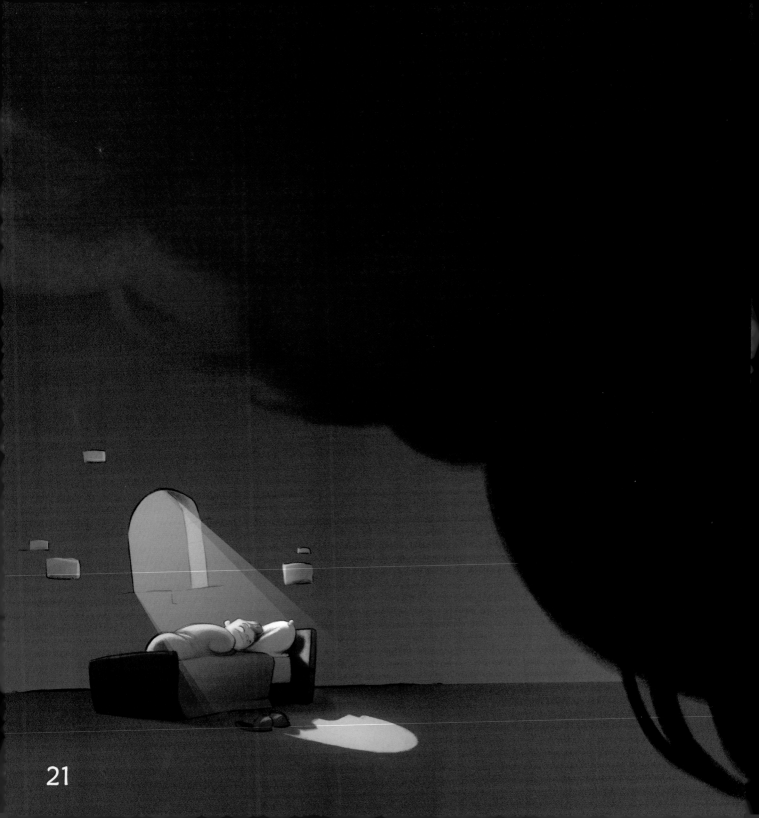

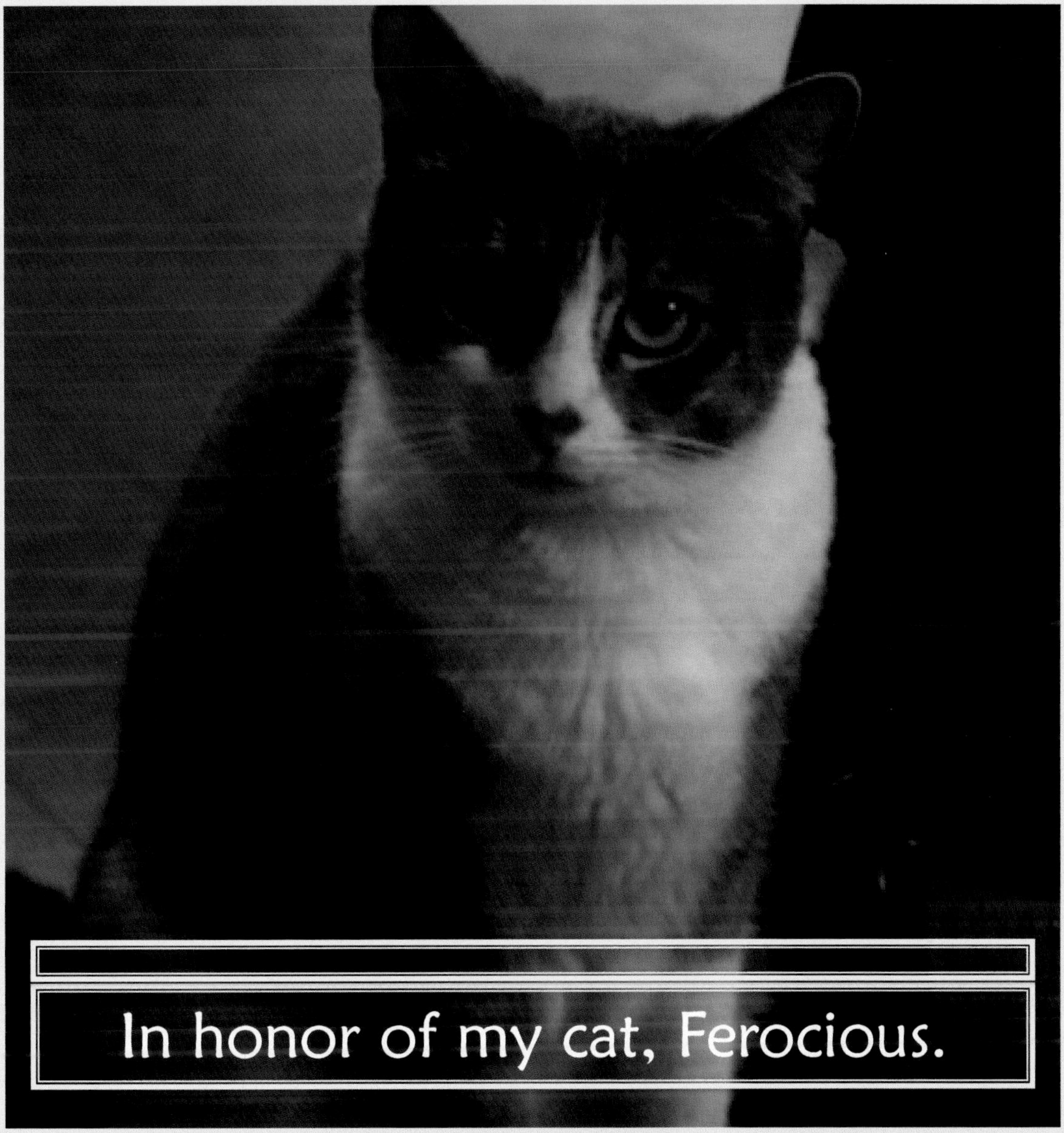

In honor of my cat, Ferocious.

nk you for being my partner, making me be accou

and for all the warm snuggles when I needed them

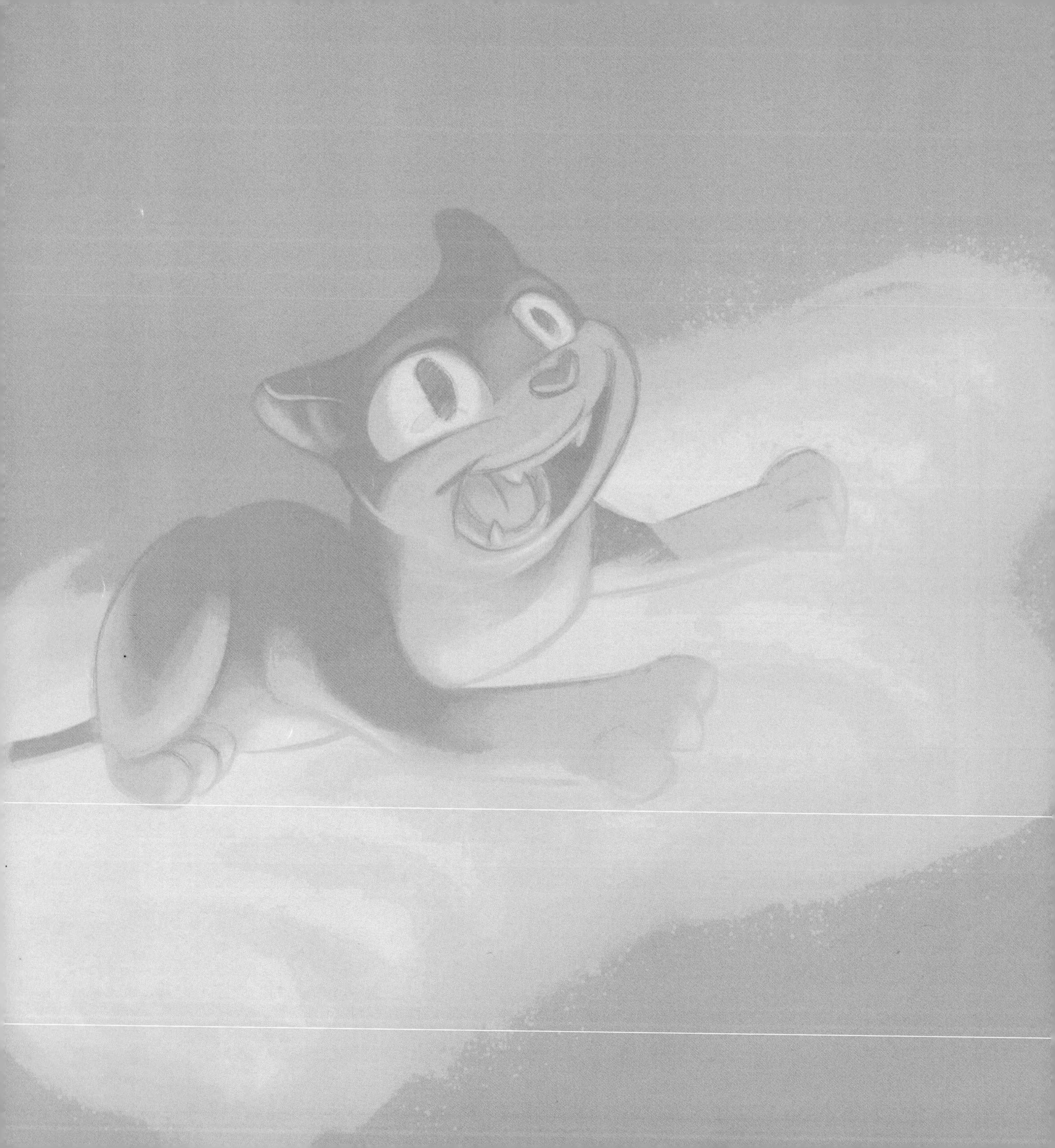